Joy to the Wolf

An Instalove Christmas Romance
Holidays with the Shifters Series
By
Rose Bak

Joy to the Wolf

Holidays With the Shifters, Volume 5

Rose Bak

Published by Rose Bak, 2021.

Table of Contents

About This Book

A wolf-shifter saying she's his fated mate? She's been there, done that, and got the divorce papers to prove it.

Joy is newly divorced and ready to start over. After her husband dumps her for his fated mate, she moves to a new town where there are other shifters around to provide support to her daughter. The little wolf shifter was always an outcast in their old pack, but in the town of Greysden no one seems to care that what kind of shifter you are or if your mother is human.

Playboy Luc knows his party days are over the minute he runs into his mate for the first time while Christmas shopping. The curvy little human already knows all about wolf shifters and fated mates, but unfortunately she was burned by her ex.

Joy is the only present Luc wants for Christmas. He's determined to prove to her that she's the only woman for him, and fortunately for him, her daughter is ready to help.

Can he convince her to take another chance at love?

About the "Shifters for the Holidays" series: The shifter town of Greysden is gearing up for the holidays and some of its sexiest residents are finally finding their true mates. The road to love isn't easy, but with a little help from fate and some nosy small-town matchmakers, there's a guaranteed happily ever after. If you love short and steamy standalone romances with curvy women and growly shifter men who fall fast and hard, this is the holiday series for you.

Download your copy of this instalove Christmas romance today!

Want a free book? Sign up for my newsletter[1] to be the first to know about new books and special sales. No spamming, I promise. Click here[2] to sign up for my newsletter and get your free book.

---

1.   https://storyoriginapp.com/giveaways/62ee758e-068f-11eb-904e-c373f6014fe1
2.   https://storyoriginapp.com/giveaways/62ee758e-068f-11eb-904e-c373f6014fe1

Keep reading after the story for a special preview of "Wolf Doctor", book one of the Bite-Sized Shifters series.

Dedication

For new starts and second chances at love.

3

Joy

"How about this one, Mommy?"

I glanced over towards my five-year-old daughter's voice. She was standing at the end of the store aisle holding up a Christmas wreath decorated with birds. It was pretty hideous, and I hid my smile. It wasn't exactly what I had in mind when we planned to decorate our new apartment.

"Is there something more festive, like something with a Christmas design? Like candy canes or presents?" I asked.

She nodded. "I'll get the other one."

I returned to looking for ornaments for the Christmas tree. I was pleased to see that this store had several aisles of Christmas decorations because I'd given all of my other ornaments to one of my neighbors in Wyoming when I moved away. I didn't want any reminders of my ex or our life together, not after everything that had happened between us.

Honestly, I was surprised that a shifter town like Greysden had embraced Christmas. There were several holiday events and every house and business in town was decorated for the holiday. The pack my ex-husband was in mostly ignored Christmas as "a human thing".

When Kelsey didn't return right away, I went looking for her in the next aisle. It must have been a mother's intuition that something was wrong, because to my horror my daughter had climbed up on the shelves. She was balancing precariously on her toes ten feet up as she tried to reach something on the highest shelf.

"Kelsey! Don't move!" I yelled as I raced down the aisle towards her.

In slow motion I saw my daughter startle, then her foot slipped of the shelf edge that she was standing on. She shrieked as she fell backwards towards the concrete floor, her long dark hair spreading out like a fan around her. I was running full out, but I knew I wouldn't make it to her in time. There was a blur of motion from the other direction and to my shock, a man who seemed to come out of nowhere caught her before she hit the floor.

I came to a complete stop a few feet away from them, my heart pounding frantically.

The man held Kelsey firmly, one thickly muscled arm underneath her thighs and one around her waist, holding her back against his broad chest.

"Hey, watch the claws there, pup," the man said quietly. "You're safe now."

I looked down and to my horror, Kelsey's claws were out. She was gripping the man's arm, breaking the skin, and causing him to bleed. Crap. We'd moved to Greysden because it was a shifter town, but as a human, I had no idea what the protocol was here. Were shifters out in the open around the humans? Was the man going to have to report her to the authorities for scratching him? She was just a little kid, she hadn't learned how to control her wolf side yet.

"Kelsey!" I hissed. "Put those things away and apologize to the nice man."

The man looked towards me for the first time, his eyes widening.

He was a big man, with wide shoulders, a trim waist, and a muscular physique. He was startlingly handsome, with olive skin, light brown hair, and a square jaw covered with just enough scruff that I had the strangest urge to feel it between my thighs. I mentally shook myself and met his intense dark eyes.

"I'm so..."

"Mine!" he interrupted with a growl. His eyes flashed, and I realized that he was some kind of a shifter. I recognized the look of animal pacing close to the surface. The possessive look he was giving me immediately put me on edge. I'd seen that look before.

"You can put her down now, thank you."

When the man didn't move, I rushed forward and grabbed my daughter out of his arms, settling her on my hip and holding her against me protectively. Kelsey wrapped her arms around my neck and snuggled closer but kept her gaze on the man. She was trembling, I realized. I wasn't sure if the man had made her uncomfortable or if she was freaked out about almost falling, but either way, I felt a strong urge to get us both out of here.

The man continued to stare at me with the most intense gaze. I had the strangest sense like I knew him from somewhere, but I couldn't figure out why he seemed so familiar. All I knew was that this situation was freaking me out.

"Thanks for helping my daughter, and I'm sorry about the scratches," I said. "Have a nice day."

"Mine!" he growled again.

What on earth was this guy talking about? I didn't want to stay to find out. I turned on my heel and practically ran towards the door, my heart pounding out of my chest.

"What about the Christmas decorations, Mommy?" Kelsey protested.

"We'll get them later," I promised. "We need to go home now."

"Wait!" The man rushed up to us as we reached the front door. He grabbed the edge of the open door. "Who are you?"

"Nobody," I said firmly as I shoved all my weight against the door to push it out of his hand so we could exit. "Goodbye."

Luc

I watched in stunned silence as my mate rushed out the door. I wasn't sure exactly what had happened. Why had she run away from me? And why was she with a shifter child when she was clearly human? The wolf pup had called her "Mommy" so clearly the woman had been in a relationship with a shifter.

She's OUR mate! My wolf growled in displeasure at the thought of any other man touching our mate.

My mate was beautiful. She had long dark hair and light brown skin, hinting at a Hispanic heritage. Her face was smooth and clear, with brown eyes and full lips that were covered in a clear gloss. She had an hourglass shape with large breasts, a small waist, and generous hips. And that ass. My god, it had been all I could not to squeeze those round globes.

I leaned back against the brick wall on the outside of the shop and watched the woman of my dreams literally run away like the hounds of hell were chasing her. The little girl watched me over her mother's shoulder. She waved and shot me a smile, and I found myself waving back.

She was adorable, and as the child of my mate, the girl was now mine too. I just needed to figure out who they were. I wasn't too worried about finding them again. Greysden was a small town, and you ran into everyone eventually.

I was still standing there thinking about what had just happened when my brother Tony walked by with his mate Marissa. They walked hand in hand, smiling at each other like fools. Those two were so in love it was almost sickening. Although I suddenly understood a little better.

"What's up bro?" Tony asked when they reached me. "You look pensive, and that's not a look I see very often on you."

"Har har," I grumbled. All our lives Tony had insisted that he was the "smart brother", and I was the "pretty brother". In reality we were both smart and good-looking, at least that's what our mother always said.

"Are you OK, Luc?" Marissa put her hand on my arm in concern, and Tony growled behind her. She turned around and smacked him on the chest. "Quit being a caveman."

When she looked at me again I shared the news.

"I just met my mate."

I could hear the wonder in my voice.

"What? Who is she? Where is she?" Marissa asked excitedly. "I always wanted a sister."

I shook my head. "I don't know. I just saw her in the store, but I guess I freaked her out because she grabbed her pup and ran away from me."

"She has a pup?" Tony asked. "So she's mated?"

I shook my head. "She's human, and her daughter is a wolf. But she's unclaimed."

I hadn't seen a mate mark on the long column of her elegant neck, nor had I sensed the blended scents of a mated pair. She was definitely unattached.

"That makes it easier," Tony responded. "It's always messy if shifters are already in a relationship when they meet their fated mate."

"What are you going to do now?" Marissa asked.

"I'm going to go see my mom. That woman's more blood hound than wolf. She'll help me find out who my mate is."

An hour later I was sitting at my mom's kitchen table, eating a roast beef sandwich while my mom made a couple calls. She'd been ecstatic when I told her that not only had I found my mate, but that she had a daughter. Mom had been dying for a grandchild.

She agreed to help me find out who my mate was and struck gold on her third call.

"Really? Oh great, yeah, that's helpful. Thanks Mr. Xenakis."

She hung up and I raised my eyebrows at her questioningly. "According to Mr. Xenakis, the woman just moved here a few days ago."

Mr. Xenakis ran the diner downtown with his wife and he was one of the biggest gossips in a town full of nosy shifters.

"They came in for breakfast yesterday and you know Mr. Xenakis, he pumped the woman for information while he was serving her. He said she's very nice, but a little guarded, and her pup is cute as a button. Very polite little girl too."

When Mom paused, I made a little "come on" motion with my hand. "So what did she say?"

"Her name is Joy. She and her daughter Kelsey just moved here from Wyoming. No word on the father, but it was clear that he's out of the picture. Joy was hinting around about shifters, trying to get information. I don't think she understands that we can tell that her child is a shifter."

I nodded. "Yeah, she's got a good set of claws on her. Do you find out where she lives?"

"Yes, she just moved into that apartment above Greysden Veterinary Hospital. Apparently she's a veterinary technician and her former employer connected her with Valerie Lupa to help her get a job here. She comes highly recommended."

Our mate is a hard worker, my wolf noted with satisfaction. *We should mate her now.*

I stood up. "I've got to get over there."

Mom's hand shot out. "Luc, your mate is human. You might want to take your time on this one. At least make a plan."

"Oh, I've got a plan. I'm going to go get my mate."

Joy

After lunch, I dropped Kelsey off at babysitter's house and headed to work. My new employer Dr. Valerie had helped me find a nice shifter woman who could keep an eye on Kelsey during the times I was at work. Mrs. Patterson ran a small daycare for shifter kids out of her home, and the older woman was well-loved in the community.

The daycare offered full day and after school support. Once Kelsey started kindergarten after the holidays one of Mrs. Patterson's staff would pick up my daughter and the other kids after school. It was the perfect arrangement for me as a working mom.

I was only scheduled for half a day today but starting tomorrow I would be on the schedule for full days. I'd worked for many years as a vet tech in Wyoming, and when I told my boss I was interested in moving to Greysden, he graciously connected me with someone he knew from vet school. Just my luck, Valerie was hiring when I called.

"Hey Joy, how are you doing today?" my new boss greeted me. She was beautiful and smart and confident – everything I aspired to be. It was only my third day of work and I already loved working here.

"Great Val, thank you."

"I'm going to have you assist me with a spay today," she told me. "You've done that before, right?"

"Of course."

I bustled around the surgical room, helping Val get set up and then bringing in the large German shepherd we'd be operating on today.

"How are you settling in here in Greysden?" Val asked.

"Pretty well, I really like it here."

Val gave me a considering glance. "I understand your daughter is a wolf shifter."

I stiffened. "Who told you that?"

Val smiled. "No one needed to tell me. I could smell her." At my curious look she explained, "Shifters can usually tell another shifter right away, just by scent."

Suddenly a conversation I'd had with Kelsey earlier made sense.

"Who was that wolf Mommy? He seemed nice," she'd asked me.

"How do you know he's a wolf?"

"I can just tell. I don't know why."

Val spoke again, drawing me out of my reverie.

"I don't know you very well yet Joy and I don't want to pry into your personal life," she began carefully. "But I imagine that as a human raising a shifter you might have questions, especially if the father's not in the picture. I just wanted to offer that if you or Kelsey need to talk about anything, I'm glad to help."

I looked at my boss. "Is it rude for me to ask what kind of shifter you are?" I asked.

"Not at all. I'm a wolf, just like Kelsey. Have you been around a lot of shifters?"

I nodded. "I lived in a shifter neighborhood with my ex," I said. "But they were pretty insular. They didn't really trust humans and I always felt like an outsider there. After my...after my divorce I realized that there was no reason to stay there. I didn't have any good friends there, and a lot of my ex-husband's pack looked down on Kelsey. They kept calling her 'half-breed' and didn't want to let her play with their kids."

My boss shook her head. "There are still a lot of shifter groups like that, unfortunately. My good friend Kat came from a pack like that. How did you find out about Greysden then?"

"There was a shifter from another pack who worked with me," I explained. "She has friends here and said Greysden was welcoming of all species, human or shifter. She said it would be a good place for me to raise Kelsey and learn how to help her when weird things happen, like today."

Val looked at me sharply. "Why, what happened today?"

"Kelsey was climbing some shelves in the store and started to fall. Some guy caught her, but she scratched him with her claws." I rushed to add, "Not on purpose."

Val shook her head. "Happens all the time with pups. They're not old enough to know how to control their shift yet. Who did she scratch?"

"I don't know, but Kelsey thought he was also a wolf."

"There are a lot of wolves here," Val responded. "The town was founded by a grey wolf pack, although it later opened up to other shifters."

Just then they heard a commotion outside. "Luc! You can't go back there!"

The door to the surgery opened and the wolf from earlier strode in, his eyes immediately latching onto me. "Mate!"

I looked at Valerie and saw her eyes widen.

"Luc, what's going on here?" she asked.

"This female is my mate. She's mine."

"This female has a name," I protested. "And there's no way I'm falling for that line again."

Luc

My mate glared at me from across the room, her eyes shooting fire. She was wearing baggy scrubs, her beautiful long hair contained on top of her hair in one of those messy buns that women seemed to like to wear. Her face was flushed with anger, and she looked so hot I felt my cock twitch in reaction.

"We're a little busy in here, Luc," Val chided me, looking pointedly at the unconscious dog on the table.

"I told him Doctor, I told him he couldn't come back, and he just blew by me."

I realized the receptionist had followed me in. I'd scarcely noticed her. The minute I entered the clinic I was so focused on finding my mate I'd developed tunnel vision.

"When do have a break, Joy?" I asked. "I need to talk to you."

Her eyes widened in surprise that I knew her name, then narrowed again. "None of your business. Please leave."

She looked at her boss. "I don't even know this guy, I swear."

"We met at the store," I contradicted her. "I rescued your daughter, remember?"

Val laughed. "Oh that was you, Luc? I hear you got scratched for your trouble."

I shrugged. "It's healed already."

"Why don't you go wait in the lobby?" Val suggested. "If Joy wants to talk to you when we're finished, I'll send her out."

I met my mate's eyes. Our gazes locked, we stared at each other in silent communication. I could see the fear in her eyes battling with annoyance and a hint of interest. I sniffed and caught a hint of her arousal. I wasn't sure what she was afraid of, especially since she was clearly familiar with shifters, but she couldn't hide her interest. Not completely.

"I'll see you in a little bit," I told her, offering my most charming smile.

Joy came out about twenty minutes later, face stony and arms crossed protectively over her chest. I stood to greet her, moving into her space, and she shot one arm out, pushing against my chest. My wolf hummed happily as she touched us.

"Whoa there wolfie, how about you show some respect for personal space?"

I stepped back and she took a deep breath. "What is so important that you interrupted me at work?"

"Now that I found you, I want to get to know you better. Can we have dinner tonight?"

"I'm working late."

"A late dinner then?"

"No, I need to pick up my daughter."

"Breakfast tomorrow? Lunch?"

She sighed. "Look, I'm sure you're a nice person but I have absolutely no interest in dating right now, especially a shifter. I'm going to suggest you go find yourself a nice little female wolf and leave me alone."

"Your daughter is a shifter."

"I'm aware of that," she said, stiffening. Her gaze turned wary as she went all "protective mama" on me. I tried to send her comforting vibes.

"So you're familiar with shifter relationships then."

"A bit," she said grudgingly. "My ex was a shifter. Obviously."

"Did he ever talk to you about fated mates?"

She laughed bitterly. "Oh yeah, he sure did."

"You're my mate." I told her, relieved that she would understand the significance of my declaration. "You and I have been matched by fate. We are destined to be together forever."

She started laughing.

"What's so funny?" I asked in confusion.

As her laughter died down, she gave me a look that was a combination of haughty and hurt. "Yeah, I've heard that one before. Done that, bought the t-shirt, as they say. I know you probably think I'm fresh meat since I'm new in town, but why don't you find some other naive human who will buy that load of crap. I've got work to do. Please don't bother me again."

"But..."

Joy gave me a glare that could strip paint. "Not interested. Leave. Me. Alone."

With one final glare, she turned on her heel and was gone.

My wolf whined inside me, confused about what had just happened.

"Yeah, I'm confused too, buddy."

I decided to make a strategic retreat. I had some work to do, so I headed over to the office. I worked as a city planner for the town of Greysden, and I'd decided to do some Christmas shopping on my lunch break. Then I'd run into my mate and had never gone back. I'd been so focused on her I hadn't even thought about work. It was just after five o'clock when I got there, so everyone else was heading home. I powered through a couple of hours of work, pushing away thoughts of my mate and concentrating on what I needed to get done after being gone all afternoon.

When I was caught up with everything I needed to finish I headed home. I had a quick dinner, then decided to let my wolf out for a run. My house, like many in Greysden, was only a short distance from the woods so I headed out on my back porch naked and called my wolf forth.

I felt my bones break and grow, and my muscles elongate as the shift happened. It was a strange combination of magical and painful. My body grew larger as fur spouted, my tail extended, and claws and fangs replaced fingers and teeth. The wolf stretched lazily, warming up his muscles, before taking off at a run.

I mostly didn't pay too much attention as he ran, my mind busy puzzling over what to do about my mate.

I guess I wasn't surprised when my wolf popped us out of the woods right behind the veterinary clinic. The clinic backed up right on the woods, with a second story apartment that was accessed from the rear. I stopped at the edge of the woods, looking up at the lit windows, knowing my mate was there.

My wolf howled piteously, sad that I wouldn't let him go up and claim his mate. With my keen shifter vision, I saw a tiny face appear in the window. Kelsey. Of course as a wolf she would sense my presence. She watched me carefully, her eyes unblinking, and I wondered if she recognized me in my wolf form.

A few minutes later I saw my mate appear behind her, looking out of the window curiously. She likely couldn't see me the way her daughter could. She looked a little confused as she stared out the window before drawing her daughter away and turning off the light.

My wolf and I stepped back into the trees and settled into a place where we could watch the apartment without drawing attention to ourselves. Resting my head on my paws, I slept through until morning.

Joy

I tossed and turned restlessly, unable to sleep. My mind was occupied with Luc. And so was Kelsey's apparently, because last night she swore that she saw his wolf hanging out in the woods.

He'd called me his mate yesterday and for a moment I'd felt the truth of his statement. That would explain the strange draw I felt towards him. But then I remembered how my ex had said the same thing to me years ago.

We'd met when he brought a stray cat into the clinic. The poor thing had been run over and Cliff felt sorry for it. We'd saved the cat and Cliff left with my number. At dinner that night he told me that he loved me. I'd scoffed at him reminding him that we'd known each other for only a few hours. Then he revealed that he was a wolf shifter. I know about shifters of course although I hadn't spent a lot of time around them.

"Shifters know their mates on site," he'd assured me. "It's fate."

He'd engaged in a charm offensive that ended up with me moving in with him and getting pregnant almost immediately. I learned that everyone in his neighborhood was part of the same "pack", and they followed an older wolf they called alpha. The alpha wasn't pleased about Cliff taking a human mate. Neither were the rest of his packmates.

When I got pregnant, and I told Cliff I wanted us to get married. None of the shifters seemed to understand what the big deal was but Cliff was pretty smitten with me, I believed that even now, so he went along with it.

The women in the pack often pointed out that he'd never bitten me to mark me as his mate. I didn't quite understand the significance, but the whole thing seemed ridiculous. I had a wedding ring and that's all I wanted.

Kelsey was born and things seemed to be going along OK with us until the day Cliff came home late one night and broke the news I'd never expected.

"There's no easy way to say this, but I found my true mate."

"What are you talking about?" I'd asked. "You said I was your true mate."

"I thought you were, but I was wrong. I guess that's why I never wanted to claim you officially."

"The biting thing?" I asked.

He nodded. "I'm sorry Joy. I care for you, I really do, so I guess I really wanted you to be my mate and convinced myself you were. But now that I've met Ashley, I can see the difference. I love her."

His words hit me like a punch to the gut.

"What are you saying?" I asked.

"I saw Ashley this morning when she came to visit the alpha. As soon as I saw her, our wolves took over and I couldn't help but claim her."

He shifted his collar, and I could see the bite on his neck. The significance of his words hit me like a punch to the solar plexus.

"Oh my god, you slept with her? A woman you just met? While you were married to me?"

He nodded. "I'm sorry, I swear I never meant to hurt you, but I can't fight fate."

"Get out!" I screamed. "Leave now!"

"I'll give you the house," he told me, like that was supposed to make it all better.

The pained look on his face told me that it wasn't easy for him to break this news to me, but I wasn't in any position to be charitable right now.

"I'll make sure that you and Kelsey are provided for, but I won't be able to see you two again. Shifter mates are very jealous, and Ashley wants us to have full-wolf cubs of our own. I know you'll take good care of my little girl."

"You're abandoning your daughter too?" I was gasping for air, incredulous that this had happened.

He winced, and I realized that I never really knew the man that I'd married. Dumping me was one thing, abandoning his daughter was despicable.

"I'm sorry," he said again. "I'll sign over custody and all the assets, and I'll pay child support so you're taken care of. Just send me the papers at the main pack house. I'm going to stay there for a while until Ashley and I get our own place on pack lands."

"Fuck you!"

He gave me a sad look and then left. That was the last time I saw my ex-husband. As soon as he was gone, I dropped to the floor crying. I was still there the next morning when Kelsey woke up.

"Hurry up, Mom!"

Kelsey pulled on my hand as we waded through the crowd at the "Skating with Santa" event. Our new town really went all out for Christmas. They'd turned the local hockey rink into a winter wonderland, complete with a giant inflatable Santa in the middle. Kids and their parents were ice skating around Santa, decked out in holiday sweaters.

I was exhausted after being up all night and then working all day, but I couldn't disappoint Kelsey. She'd been begging to attend "Skating with Santa" ever since she heard about the event. We got in line for skate rentals, and I reminded my daughter that I hadn't skated since I was a kid.

"Don't worry Mommy, we'll both learn together."

I had my doubts. Unlike my daughter, I had very little natural athleticism. She took after her dad in that way. As if she could read my mind, Kelsey asked, "Do you think Daddy will call me for Christmas?"

We hadn't heard from Cliff directly in the six months since he'd wrecked our world. He'd never even said goodbye to Kelsey, and for that I could never forgive him. When the other wolves in our pack had given us shit about Kelsey being a "half breed" he was always the first to defend her, but one night with his new mate had changed his mind quick. I'd never realized my ex was such a selfish coward.

I leaned down to meet Kelsey's serious gaze. "I'm sorry sweetie, but Daddy is busy with his new family now. I don't think we'll hear from him."

I'd heard from the rumor mill that he'd gotten his mate pregnant pretty much the day he met her. I imagined he'd have his full blood kid pretty soon.

"I don't understand why he doesn't want us anymore," Kelsey sniffed. It was a conversation we'd had many times over the last six months.

"I don't understand either," I told her. "Just remember that Mommy loves you and I'll always be here for you, no matter what. I promise." I reached out and did the "pinkie swear" with her to show how serious I was, even as I fought back my own tears.

I was glad that we reached the front of the line so we could drop the subject. I paid for our skates and then we moved over to a bench to put them on. I was leaning over and struggling with my laces when I felt a shiver run down my spine right before I heard a deep voice behind me.

"Ladies."

Luc

It was a stroke of luck running into my mate today. I'd spent the night outside her apartment making sure she and her pup were safe, then headed home to change so I do a shift at the refreshment stand with my mother. Mom was famous for volunteering us boys for things. It was annoying although her volun-telling us stuff was exactly how my brother Tony had met his mate.

Mom and I were heading back to the parking lot when I scented my mate and abruptly changed directions, my mother in tow.

Mate! Our mate is here! Find her now.

I followed her scent to a bench on the side of the skating rink.

"Ladies."

My mate jumped at the sound of my voice. Kelsey was all suited up for skating, but Joy was still trying to lace up her skates, fingers fumbling with the knots.

"Allow me," I said, dropping down to my knees in front of her. I ran my hands down her shapely calves and she shivered. I knew she felt the same sense of awareness as I did from our nearness.

"I'm fine," she protested.

I ignored her and started working on the knots in the laces.

"How are you today, pup?" I asked Kelsey with a smile.

The little girl gave me a smile. "I'm fine, thank you." She had nice manners.

"We didn't officially meet yesterday, but my name is Luc, and this here is my mom, Ida." I nodded towards my mother. "You're Kelsey, right?"

Kelsey nodded.

"Mom, this is Kelsey and Joy, they're new to town. I met them yesterday."

"Welcome to Greysden," my mom said warmly. "I've heard so much about you. You girls will have to come to Sunday dinner tomorrow."

Yes, bring our mate and her pup to the den, my wolf encouraged.

Joy looked alarmed. "Oh, that's very nice of you but we're pretty busy."

"Nonsense. I'm sure Luc will bring you to meet the rest of the family soon."

"Is everyone in your family a wolf, Mr. Luc?" Kelsey asked curiously.

I shook my head. "No, my brother and my uncle both are mated with humans like your mom."

"Do you have a mate?" the girl asked.

I looked at Joy, but she was studiously avoiding my gaze. "I'm working on it."

"Do you want to skate with us?"

"Mr. Luc is very busy," Joy answered for me. She stood up and grabbed Kelsey's hand. "Nice to meet you Ida, I'm sure we'll see you around."

She rushed off, tugging Kelsey behind her.

"You're going to go skate with them, aren't you?" Mom asked as we watched them race away.

"Of course."

"All right, you be sure to bring them to Sunday dinner tomorrow to meet the family." She leaned up and kissed my cheek. "Good luck."

It didn't take long for me to rent my own pair of skates and head out onto the ice. Joy was nervously hugging the wall, but Kelsey seemed to be getting the hang of it pretty quickly.

"I think we need to go faster, Mommy," Kelsey said. "See?" She let go of Joy's hand and glided away a bit, then came back. The girl clearly scented me coming because she turned around and gave me a welcoming smile before her mother realized I was there.

"Do you need a hand?" I asked.

"We're fine."

Joy jumped at the sound of my voice and almost wiped out. I reached for her hand, the one that wasn't gripping the wall. The minute our skin touched, I felt a current of electricity run up my arm. Judging by Joy's soft gasp, she felt it too. My cock twitched.

"Why don't you take your mom's other hand, and we can both help her, pup?" I suggested.

Kelsey glided over to the other side, forcing Joy to let go of the wall. The three of us started skating slowly around the rink, and after a few minutes, my mate seemed to relax and be more comfortable. We all picked up speed.

"Mommy, can I go skate with Santa and those kids?" Kelsey asked, pointing to where someone dressed as Santa was skating with a long line of younger kids.

Joy nodded. "OK honey but do not leave this rink without me, do you understand?"

"Yes Mommy." The girl took off towards the group of little kids on the other side of the rink.

Joy laughed ruefully. "It's her first time and she's already a pro. She seems to have a natural balance that I don't have."

"It's a shifter thing," I assured her. The two of us picked up speed a bit and were gliding along nicely. My wolf was curled up in my mind happy that we were doing something with our mate. "But you're getting there."

"It's been a while. I haven't done this since I was her age," she explained.

The longer we skated, the more comfortable Joy seemed to become. I kept expecting her to pull her hand out of mine, but she seemed content to stay connected. Maybe it was because she felt safer skating that way, but I hoped it was because she liked holding hands with me as much as I did with her.

We chatted easily as we circled the rink, getting to know each other a bit. I kept the conversation superficial, not wanting to freak her out.

When I sensed that she was getting tired, I pulled her off onto a bench where she could rest and still keep an eye on Kelsey.

Joy shivered, feeling the cold more now that we weren't moving. I put my arm around her, pulling her into my side. She fit there perfectly, and my wolf practically purred with happiness.

She started to pull away from me, but I tightened my grip. "Just relax."

"You know telling someone to relax usually has the opposite effect, right?"

I turned to meet her annoyed gaze. "Maybe I'll try something else then."

Joy

Luc leaned in and before I could guess his intentions, his lips were on mine. They were strong and soft and a little cold from being outside. His arm was circled around my shoulders, keeping me close, as he pressed his cold lips against mine.

I felt an immediate surge of something, excitement or awareness I guess, and I gasped. He took advantage of my parted lips and his tongue thrust into the depths of my mouth. All coherent thought stopped in my mind. I circled his tongue with mine, dueling for control.

Luc shifted to face me more fully, wrapping his leg on the outside of mine and pulling me closer. My hands, having a mind of their own, slid under his open jacket, exploring the muscled planes of his back while he made love to my mouth. This guy could really kiss.

I could feel my nipples hardening painfully against the fabric of my bra as the kiss went on and on. Luc finally dragged his mouth away, kissing his way down my jaw to my neck. He nipped me, pulling the flesh at the bottom of my neck between his teeth, and it was enough to jolt me out of my stupor. I suddenly realized we were necking in a public place full of children.

"Luc. Stop," I gasped as I pushed against his chest. To his credit, he pulled back immediately, although he kept his arms wrapped around me. We watched each other, both of us breathing hard as we caught our breath.

"Mommy!"

I heard Kelsey call my name and pulled away from Luc guiltily. Kelsey was on the other side of the short wall that separated our bench from the rink. "I'm hungry."

One thing about having a shifter child, they were always hungry.

I stood up, purposely avoiding Luc's gaze. "OK honey, let's go home and get something to eat."

"Can Mr. Luc come?" she asked.

I repressed a sigh. "Mr. Luc was just going." I turned to him and shot him a stern look. "Right?"

We stared at each other for a long moment before he turned to my daughter and gave her a smile. "I do have to go, pup, but I'll see you for dinner tomorrow OK? I'll pick you guys up at quarter to six."

"I didn't agree to dinner," I hissed at him, conscious of my daughter watching the exchange.

Luc moved closer. "Come on Mate, my mother will never let me hear the end of it if I don't bring you."

"We're not going to dinner," I whisper-shouted back.

"OK, you leave me no choice," he said as he walked away. "I'll have to bring in the big guns. See you later Kelsey."

A few hours later my cell phone rang. Kelsey was coloring while I read a book on the couch. I didn't recognize the number, so I answered cautiously.

"Hello?"

"Hello Joy, dear, it's Ida. Luc's mother. We met earlier today."

I repressed a sigh. "I remember. But how did you get this number?"

"It's a small town," she responded, like that explained everything. Which it didn't, because I was pretty sure that Val was the only person in town with my number.

"I've been thinking about your adorable little girl, and I think it would be nice for her to hang out with some other wolves."

"This whole town is full of wolves," I answered.

"There's a lot of different shifters here, dear, but I understand that it can be hard for a human parent to explain to their dual-natured children about their animal side. That's why you should come for dinner tomorrow."

"Excuse me?" I asked, not seeing the connection.

"The boys can shift with her and play in the yard for a while. They can help her learn more about shifting."

"The boys?"

"Luc and my other son Tony. And you can talk to Marissa about what it's like to give birth to a shifter as a human. She's going to be pregnant soon, I just know it."

"Marissa?"

"Tony's mate. It'll be nice to have all the mates together. I mean, I wondered about Luc ever finding his, he's so damned stubborn, but I guess I shouldn't have worried because he recognized you the minute he saw you."

"But, I'm not..."

"You're not a vegetarian, are you dear?"

"What? No." I was having a hard time keeping up with this conversation.

"Great. I'm making a roast. It can be tricky to find my house if you haven't been here before, so I'll have Luc pick you up at five forty-five."

"Look, Ida I appreciate the invitation, but..."

"Of course dear, it's the least I can do to welcome you to our town."

"I'm sorry but..."

"See you tomorrow night." The phone clicked off and I stared at it in confusion. What had just happened?

"Mommy?" Kelsey was watching me curiously. "Are we doing to Miss Ida's for dinner?"

I frowned. "How did you know it was her?"

She pointed at one ear. "Shifter hearing. I'm so excited. I can't wait to play with the other wolves."

Luc

Was it sneaky of me to sic my mother on Joy? Absolutely. Was I sorry? Not at all.

When I pulled up to the lot behind the veterinary clinic Joy and Kelsey were waiting for me outside. Joy was carrying a box that looked like it came from the bakery up the street. I parked and went around to open the door for Kelsey, making sure she was buckled in tight in the backseat. It was only a five minute drive, but better safe than sorry.

Joy slid into the front seat next to me and I gave her a smile. "I'm glad you decided to come, Mate."

"Stop calling me that," she hissed. "And don't play innocent with me, mister. I know you sicced your mother on me."

"She is very convincing," I laughed. Joy just glared at me. "You'll have fun, I promise."

We made the short drive to my mom's house in silence, but as we exited the car, Joy pulled me aside before we opened the door for Kelsey.

"Are you sure that...I mean, is your family going to have a problem with Kelsey?" she whispered.

I wrinkled my forehead in confusion. "What do you mean? Why would they have a problem?"

"Because she's not full wolf."

"What difference does that make?" I asked in confusion.

She gave me a warning look. "OK, but if one person in there refers to my child as a half-breed, I'm out of there."

I reared back in shock. "What? Who did that?"

My wolf growled, upset that anyone would insult the pup who was part of our mate and therefore under our protection.

"Everyone in my ex-husband's pack," she bit off. "They weren't happy about his relationship with me, and they certainly never accepted my daughter. They said we polluted their wolf bloodline."

My wolf growled again, agitated that our mate was hurt. I lifted my hand to her shoulder and met her eye. "We don't have that prejudice here," I told her solemnly. "Everyone is going to love her, not only because she's a cool kid, but also because she's my mate's pup."

She still looked a little wary, but I figured seeing was believing. I clapped her shoulder. "Come on, let's get inside."

As soon as we got inside, Kelsey and Joy were greeted like old friends. Joy was dragged into the kitchen by my mom so she could meet Marissa and Sarah, my uncle's mate.

Tony and my Uncle Hank were playing a video game in the living room, but they immediately stopped when I walked in with Kelsey.

"Well, hello pup," Uncle Hank boomed. "You must be the pretty little wolf that Luc told us about."

Kelsey blushed and put her hand out to shake. "It's a pleasure to meet you."

After a few minutes of small talk, it was clear that the child was comfortable with us. "Do you want to go into the back yard and let our wolves play?" I asked her.

Her eyes widened. "Yes!" she said eagerly. "But not too rough please. I'm littler than you."

I patted her head fondly. "We'll be careful, I promise. Let's just check with your mom and make sure it's OK with her."

We filed into the kitchen, Kelsey skipping ahead. "Mommy! Mommy! They want to play as wolves! Can I?"

Joy looked up from chopping vegetables, her gaze hesitant.

"She'll be fine, dear," my mom reassured her. "We can see them through the window if you want to watch them."

"OK but be careful Kelsey." Her words were spoken to her daughter but the pointed look in my direction let me know that they were intended for me. I gave my mate a reassuring smile.

We headed into the backyard with the pup. "Can you shift on command yet?" Hank asked as he knelt in front of her.

Kelsey shook her head. "My daddy tried to show me, but it didn't work. I don't know how it happens but if I get mad or sad then my wolfie comes by herself."

Hank nodded. "It's good you're here then, we can help you control your wolf better. It's hard to learn."

"Really?"

"Yeah. You should have seen Luc when he was a pup, he was always shifting at the wrong time, making a mess of things."

She giggled.

"Let's try this, sweetheart," he suggested. "I'm going to hold up this here towel so you have some privacy, then you can get out of your clothes, so you don't rip them. Wrap yourself in the towel. Tony is going to do the same thing. We'll go one-by-one and help you, how does that sound?"

"OK," she said.

Shifters normally didn't care much about nudity but given that the child was young and clearly didn't have a lot of experience with the shifter world, it was good that my uncle had thought to give her some privacy.

Once she and Tony had changed into towels, Hank gave his instructions. "Now here's what you two are going to do," he said, pointing between her and Tony. "You have to learn to be friends with your wolf. I want you to close your eyes and call to your wolf."

"What should I say?" she asked, wrinkling her brow.

"Ask your wolf does she want to come out and play with us. If she says yes, then take a deep breath in and blow it out slowly. As you blow it out, imagine that your wolf is coming out and hopefully, she will," Hank explained. "Then when you are ready to come back to your human form, you are going to do the same thing. Take a deep breath and imagine your human form. Does that make sense?"

"Yes Mr. Hank."

Hank shot me a smile over his shoulder. He really was good with kids for someone who never had any of his own.

"OK let's see if you and Tony can do it at the same time. Ready...set...go."

The pup took a deep breath, screwed her eyes closed, and blew it out slowly. To my surprise, the air shimmered around her, and she shifted on her first try. The towel dropped, revealing an adorable little grey wolf. The pup raced around in excited circles.

Tony had also shifted, and he lay on his stomach on the grass, showing the pup he was no threat. Kelsey walked around him, sniffing him curiously.

"OK Kelsey, now Luc and I are going to shift to our wolves so we can all play," Hank told her, "But if you want to stop or your get scared, just take a breath and imagine your human form so you can shift back."

I took a deep breath, just like Hank and my dad had taught me when I was Kelsey's age, and I called my wolf forward. As soon as I had shifted, Kelsey came by me, nudging me with her nose to indicate that she wanted to play.

I did a play bow, and she emulated me, then we started chasing each other around the yard. Tony and Hank joined us as we ran and rolled around in my mom's large backyard, showing Kelsey how to play. Wolves tended to play hard, but each of us took care to be gentle with the little pup.

Mate! Mate!

My wolf caught Joy's scent as soon as she stepped on the porch. Her worried gaze cleared as she saw Kelsey prancing around trying to grab Tony's tail in her mouth.

"Wow," she whispered. Despite there being three full grown almost identical looking wolves in the yard, her eyes went right to me, as if she knew me. My wolf puffed up happily. "Thank you, Luc."

Joy

My eyes filled with tears as I saw Kelsey happily playing in the yard with the larger male wolves. In the past when my daughter played with other wolves, they were always either too rough, trying to dominate her, or they ignored her altogether since she wasn't "pure".

I'd never seen Kelsey's wolf look so happy. Even though I wasn't a wolf myself, I could clearly see how much fun she was having. My eyes found Luc. I wasn't sure how I knew it was him when he looked almost exactly like the other three males, but somehow I could easily pick him out of the group.

"Thank you, Luc."

He walked over slowly, then nudged my leg with his big grey head. I stroked between his ears, amazed at how soft his fur felt. I'd seen my ex and his pack in their wolf forms enough to not be afraid, but somehow this felt different. I had the strangest urge to curl up on the ground and lay my head on his furry body. I didn't want to examine too closely why I felt so comfortable with him already.

Kelsey ran up to us, shifting to her human form mid-stride, and jumped into my arms.

"Mommy! Mommy! Did you see me shift? Mr. Hank showed me how to do it when I'm not mad or scared." She looked super proud of herself.

"That's great honey. Good job." She preened under my praise. "Ms. Ida sent me to tell you all that dinner is ready now. I bet you worked up a good appetite."

She nodded. "I did. I was chasing and chasing them, it was so much fun."

I sent Hank a grateful smile as I helped Kelsey put on her clothes, then averted my eyes as the males shifted back to human and got dressed. I wasn't used to seeing a bunch of naked men, especially a group like this.

They were all well-built and incredibly handsome, even the older wolf Hank.

We filed into the house for dinner, with Luc sitting on one side and Kelsey on the other.

While we'd finished preparing dinner I'd had a great conversation with Ida, Marissa, and Sarah, who was both Marissa's mother and Hank's mate. As the guys joined us and we sat around the table to eat, I realized that I felt more at home with this group of virtual strangers than I ever had in my old life with Cliff.

After my experience with my husband's pack, I was amazed at how the two human women fit right in with the shifters in the group. There didn't seem to be any of the power dynamics or alpha bullshit or disdain towards humans like I was used to. Everyone was laughing and talking over each other, and my daughter and I seemed to fit right in.

I was seated between Kelsey and Luc, and throughout dinner I could feel the heat of Luc's body next to mine. At some point he seemed to move closer, and his leg pressed against mine. Everywhere our bodies touched vibrated, and I could feel the attraction between us ramping up despite my efforts to ignore it. He was super solicitous throughout dinner, making sure that both Kelsey and I got enough to eat.

I laughed as my daughter took her third serving of roast from Luc. "Where are you putting all that food, Kelsey?"

"Shifting takes a lot of calories," Ida explained. "Especially when they're still growing."

I realized that I could learn a lot about my daughter's experience from Ida and resolved to make a list of questions. Maybe I could take her out for coffee and ask all the questions I'd been afraid to ask anyone in Cliff's pack. I'd felt instantly comfortable with Ida, despite the way she'd bullied me into coming for dinner.

By the time we finished dinner and got everything cleaned up, Kelsey was getting heavy lidded. All that running around and shifting had taken a lot out of her.

"We'd better get you home kiddo."

We thanked Ida and headed to the car. It was a short drive back to our place, maybe five minutes, but Kelsey was fast asleep by the time we got there. Her head was thrown back on the seat and she was snoring like a trucker.

"I'll carry her up," Luc offered quietly. "No sense waking her up."

He unbuckled her and pulled her carefully into his arms. I won't lie: my ovaries spasmed at the site of the big handsome man cradling my daughter like she was the most precious thing in the world. Luc followed me up the stairs to our apartment over the vet clinic. Once inside, we worked together to take off her shoes and socks and tuck her into bed. The poor kid never even stirred.

"Where do you sleep?" Luc asked curiously as we closed the door and exited the bedroom. "There's only one bedroom."

I couldn't help but wonder why he was familiar with my apartment. Had he dated a previous resident? I tamped down the flash of jealousy that hit me at that thought.

"I sleep in the living room. The couch is a pull-out." It wasn't comfortable, but I figured I could make do until my old house sold and we could buy something of our own here in Greysden.

Luc raised his eyebrows curiously but didn't say anything. We stood there in the hallway staring at each other awkwardly for a long moment as the atmosphere became charged, then suddenly we leapt at each other. I couldn't say who moved first, but one minute we were standing there, and the next our lips crashed together in a frantic kiss. Luc walked me backwards until I hit the wall, trapping me between the hardness of his body and the plaster.

The kiss went on and on, and every nerve ending in my body was on fire. I'd convinced myself that my first kiss with Luc at the ice skating rink was just a fluke; there was no way a kiss could be that good. But I was wrong. If anything, this kiss was even better.

I wrapped one leg around Luc's calf so that I could press my needy core against him. Understanding my intention, he grabbed my thighs and boosted me up as if I weighed nothing. I rolled my pelvis against his, seeking the pressure that my body craved.

"Hold on," Luc instructed.

I wrapped my arms around his neck, and he moved away from the wall, carrying me to the couch. He dropped to the cushions and settled me on his lap, straddling him.

I leaned forward and kissed him again. I'd promised myself I wouldn't encourage Luc, yet I couldn't seem to stop myself. I was dry humping him like a horny teenager, digging my fingernails into his broad shoulders while I rocked my pelvis against him, seeking relief. It had been a long time since I'd had sex, at least a year, and I felt a little frantic for an orgasm that wasn't self-administered.

Luc snaked one hand up beneath my shirt and squeezed my breast in his big hand. I moaned against his mouth, and he repeated the motion. His other hand slid up my thigh, underneath the plain cotton skirt I'd worn to dinner. I gasped against his mouth as I felt his fingers slide along the damp crotch of my panties.

"You're so wet for me," he whispered against my lips. "Let me give you pleasure, Mate."

He rubbed his fingers across my cloth-covered seam again and I whined, "Please Luc."

"You've got to be quiet," he reminded me as his lips caught mine again.

Meanwhile he slid my panties to one side and without warning, slid one long finger into my channel. I moaned at the invasion. Luc began pumping his finger in and out a few times, before adding a second finger. I shamelessly fucked his fingers, seeking the relief I hadn't even known I needed until I first saw him.

He bent his fingers, brushing against my G-spot just as his thumb found the swollen bundle of nerves at my apex, and suddenly I was coming. Hard. His other hand moved from my breast to tightly grip my hip to hold me still as he continued to pump his fingers inside me and apply pressure to my clit. Luc swallowed my moans with his mouth as I shivered and shook and rolled my hips against him, riding out the most powerful orgasm of my life.

When it was over I slumped against his shoulder, shivering and shaking and gasping for breath. After a few minutes I pushed back up to seated Luc and removed his fingers from my channel, bringing them to his mouth so that he could lick my essence off his fingers.

"Delicious."

It was hot as hell. I swear I almost came again just watching that.

"Oh. My. God." I gasped.

Luc shot me a satisfied smile. "I know. I've heard that everything is better when you're with your mate, but I didn't realize how much better."

I stiffened. "I wish you'd quit calling me that."

"I'll keep saying it until you believe me."

Needing distance, I slid off his lap to sit on couch next to Luc. My eyes widened as I took in the enormous bulge straining against my pants. Oh crap, I'd been so focused on my own orgasm I hadn't thought about what he needed.

"Oh, um, sorry. We should..."

Luc followed my gaze and shook his head. "Not until you're ready for more, Mate. And not when your daughter is here, and you don't have a locking door."

My eyes widened. My god, I'd been so overcome with passion that I'd totally forgotten that Kelsey was here.

"I'd better go," he said softly. I looked at him in surprise. I figured I'd have to shove him out kicking and screaming, especially after what had just happened.

He leaned forward and kissed me softly on the lips. "I'll talk to you tomorrow. Lock the door behind me, OK Mate?"

Luc

Walking away from Joy might have been the hardest thing I'd ever done. But there was no way I was going to claim her on the living room couch, especially when she wasn't ready to accept that we were mates yet.

My brother and my uncle had just found their mates recently, both of them human like Joy, and it had taken some convincing for them to get their females on-board with the mating thing. Relationships moved much more slowly in the human world. My mate was different in that she knew more about our ways and understood what mates were, yet she didn't seem to trust the concept of fated mates.

It didn't take a genius to read between the lines and figure out someone had falsely claimed she was their mate before, likely Kelsey's father. I wondered what had happened with that relationship; I'd hinted around yesterday but Joy hadn't responded. I needed to find out what happened, so I knew what I was up against.

My opportunity came faster than I would have expected. I stopped by to see my mate at the vet clinic the next morning, intending to ask her out for coffee, and found Kelsey sitting in the lobby, coloring at a table they'd set up for kids. She scented me the minute I walked in the door and ran towards me to give me an enthusiastic hug. My heart swelled with affection for the little wolf.

"Mr. Luc!"

We must move her and our mate into the den and give the pup a brother, my wolf instructed.

"Hey pup, what are you doing here?"

"Mrs. Patterson got sick, and Mommy said I could stay here with Ms. Angela," she said, nodding her head to the older woman who staffed the reception desk in the mornings.

"Good morning Angela, is Joy available?" I called.

"I'll check."

I sat down and colored with Kelsey for about five minutes before Joy came out, dressed in scrubs again and wearing her dark hair in another messy topknot. She looked adorable.

"Good morning, Mate." She narrowed her eyes at me. "I was hoping you could go get a cup of coffee with me?"

She shook her head. "Sorry, we're short staffed today and I'm booked with appointments all morning."

"I'll go for coffee with you, Mr. Luc," Kelsey offered. She shot me a hopeful look. Poor kid was probably bored to death sitting in the lobby all day.

Before Joy could respond I said, "I would love that, if your mom agrees. We could bring her back a coffee since she can't take a break." I was eager to do anything that brought me closer to my mate, plus I really liked Kelsey.

Joy shot me a look that said she knew exactly what I was doing, but then she saw the eager look on her daughter's face and relented.

"OK, but you stay right next to Mr. Luc, OK Kelsey? No wandering off. No talking to strangers. No asking him to buy you anything." She ticked the instructions off on her fingers with the air of someone who'd had this conversation before. "And you hold on tight to his hand when you cross the street."

"I promise, Mommy."

Kelsey grabbed my hand and we walked down the street to the Bearly Beans coffee shop. A bear shifter named Charlie was working at the counter. I didn't know him too well, but I'd gone to school with his older brother and in Greysden no one was a stranger.

"Who's your friend, Luc?" he asked, smiling at my companion.

"I'm Kelsey."

"Hi Kelsey, I'm Charlie. What would you like to have today? Wait, don't tell me, how about a peppermint hot chocolate?"

"Yes please. That sounds yummy."

"How about you Luc?"

"Do you know what kind of coffee your mommy likes?" I asked Kelsey, suddenly realizing that I hadn't asked.

"She likes a capra-cheenio."

"One cappuccino and one black coffee please."

Charlie hustled off to make our drinks and Kelsey tugged on my hand. "Is he a bear?" she whispered curiously.

"Yes, he is," I whispered back, even though I knew Charlie could hear us.

"I never saw a bear before," she said solemnly.

"He's a nice bear," I reassured her.

Charlie finished our drinks and Kelsey and I sat down at one of the tables. She was quiet for about ten seconds before she went in for the kill.

"Are you in love with my mommy, Mr. Luc? Is she gonna be your new mate?"

I nearly choked on my coffee, but I guess I wasn't surprised. Kelsey was a shifter, and she would have picked up on the growing mate bond between me and her mother, even if she didn't understand what it was.

"I like your mom a lot," I hedged.

"It's good for her to get a new boyfriend. I think she likes you too. You could be mates."

My wolf puffed up proudly inside me.

"Yeah? Why do you think that?"

"Mommy has been sad since my daddy left but when she smiles more when she's with you."

I saw my opening and took it, not caring that I was pumping a little kid for information.

"What happened to your daddy? Are you parents divorced?"

She nodded solemnly. "Daddy found his real mate. He thought his mate was Mommy but then he changed his mind. He told her he was wrong, and that his mate is really another lady."

"Another lady?"

"I never met her." Kelsey's eyes filled with tears. "Daddy said the new lady doesn't want me to be part of their family because I'm a half-breed and he doesn't want to make her mad. She only wants real wolves for kids."

"He told you that?" I asked angrily, my wolf and I both feeling protective of this little girl.

"No, but I heard him telling my mom that when I got up to go to the bathroom one night. Mommy was crying and then when I woke up, Daddy was gone. She said he was never coming back no more."

Jesus Christ. I wanted to find Joy's ex and beat him senseless.

"Mr. Luc, I thought when us shifters find our mates our wolves tell us that's the one we love."

"Yeah, that's true."

"Then how come Daddy's wolf made a mistake?"

"I don't know Kelsey, but I'm very sorry that happened to you and your mom."

"It's OK, I like it better here anyway, everyone is much nicer to me."

"I'm glad." I nodded towards her glass. "I've got to get back to work now, should we take that coffee to your mom?"

Joy

"Do you want to do something this weekend?"

It was Thursday night and for the fifth night in a row, Kelsey and I had spent the evening with Luc. I couldn't even say how it had happened. We'd gone to his mother's for dinner Sunday, then when he and Kelsey brought me coffee at work on Monday, he'd invited us to come to his house for dinner. My daughter had been so excited about going to his house I hadn't had the heart to refuse.

We'd eaten together every night since, at either his house or mine. Something else we'd done every night: make out like horny teenagers on my couch once Kelsey was tucked into bed. Luc would work me up into a frenzy of need, then remind me that we weren't alone and leave for the night. It was diabolical.

At this point I was so strung out with wanting him that all he had to do was look at me and my panties were wet. I'd never wanted any man as much as I wanted him. It was all I could think of, and my vibrator was a poor substitute.

Between our nights together and the way we'd been texting back and forth throughout the day, I'd gotten to know Luc pretty well. He was surprisingly deep, despite his charming demeanor, and well educated. When we weren't flirting with each other we talked about everything from books to politics to the differences between human and shifter culture.

Somewhere over the past few days I'd started to like him. I liked him a lot, and I was increasingly desperate to get closer to him. But something held me back, and it wasn't just the presence of my five-year-old daughter in the house. My feelings for him were growing quickly and it scared me to death. I'd let myself get swept away in a love-at-first-sight fantasy once before, and it didn't end well.

I wanted some space to process my emotions, yet I felt powerless to stay away from Luc. I just wished he'd stop calling me his mate and pressing me for more. Every time he talked about us getting married or having pups or even officially being in a relationship, I felt myself breaking out in hives.

It wasn't just him either, everywhere I went in town people referenced me being Luc's mate. The whole town seemed to be filled with nosy matchmakers who acted confused about why I didn't just jump into a relationship with him. Of course, that was a nice change from my old town where the shifters were all appalled at the idea of me being with one of them.

Several people had also pointed out Luc's playboy history. Apparently he'd sowed his share of wild oats, and I couldn't help but wonder if he could really give all that up for me. Instinctively I felt like I could trust Luc when he called me his mate, but I was still smarting from unexpectedly getting dumped by the last guy I thought I could trust. It felt different with Luc, there was no way I would deny that, yet I was still nervous.

"We're going to Denver tomorrow afternoon," I said, finally answering his question.

"Denver? What for?"

"My house back in Wyoming finally sold. I have to go to the title company to sign the papers they sent here, then go to the bank and take care of a few other errands."

"Kelsey is coming too?"

"Yeah, my parents actually live outside of Denver and she's going to spend the weekend with them."

"Is the house you sold the house you owned with your husband?" he asked.

I nodded. "Yeah, he signed it over in the divorce, but it was harder than I expected to sell it. It backs right up on wolf pack territory. The humans don't like to live that close to the wolves, and the wolves don't like to live off of pack property."

"Why didn't you guys live with the pack?" he asked. "I know those old school packs prefer to have everyone in one place under the alpha's watchful eye."

"I wasn't welcome there since I was human," I explained. "The pack was upset that Cliff was diluting their pure wolf blood by mating a human, so my ex negotiated that we would live next door to the pack lands instead. Once we separated, he moved back to the pack house."

"When he found his true mate?"

My eyes widened. "How did you know that?"

He nodded in the direction of the bedroom. "Kelsey".

"She knows about that?"

"She overheard you and your ex talking. She never mentioned it?"

"No, but this explains why she never asked why we split up." I nodded as several things fell into place in my mind. "She gets sad that he doesn't contact her, but never asked what happened. That explains a lot."

"So he told you that you were his mate, but then realized he was wrong?"

I nodded.

"Do you still love him?" he asked me, his expression surprisingly vulnerable.

I shook my head. "In retrospect I don't know that I ever loved him," I responded honestly. "When I met him I'd just turned thirty and I was having a little mid-life crisis thinking I was never going to get married or have kids. Then here comes Cliff and he's good looking and charming with all his sweet words about mates and love at first sight and I, well, I got swept away in the fairy tale of it all."

Luc nodded but didn't respond.

"I knew I wasn't happy in my marriage, but at least I was content. After Kelsey was born we were more like friends than husband and wife, but we never fought or anything, so I thought everything was fine. Until the night he told me he was wrong, and I wasn't his mate after all."

Luc took my hand, engulfing my smaller hand in his. "Thank you for sharing that. It helps explain why you're so resistant to the idea of the two of us being mates."

"I like you a lot Luc, but as a human, all I have to go on is what you tell me," I explained. "I know you believe we're mates, and I even believe that you have feelings for me already, but it might just be a strong attraction. What if you're wrong and you realize later that we're not really mates?"

"I've heard Marissa and Sarah say that even though they're human, they could still feel the pull of the mate bond. I don't think it was as strong as what we shifters feel, but it's definitely there," he said. "They likened it to the most intense crush they've ever had."

I reared back in surprise. Was this why I couldn't get Luc out of my mind? I thought about him all day and dreamed about him all night. I felt the oddest sense of peace when we were together, and when we weren't, I found myself imagining scenarios that would allow me to spend more time with him. In retrospect, I'd never felt that way about my husband, not even in the beginning. Could this mate thing actually be real?

As much as I tried to deny it, I had to admit that I did feel a strong pull towards him and, if I was being totally honest, I felt something that felt a lot like love. But that was impossible right? We'd only known each other for a little over a week. Yet my feelings for Luc were more intense than anything I'd ever felt for my ex, or any other man I'd dated for that matter.

Luc was watching me closely, and something in him seemed to relax. "You do feel it, don't you?" he asked, with a tone of wonder in his voice.

I stared into his eyes for a long moment before I finally admitted the truth to both myself and him. "I do."

I made a decision: I was going to trust my heart and trust Luc. I still didn't know if I believed all this fated mate talk, but I definitely wanted to give this relationship a try. Even if we weren't mates, there was no reason we couldn't just date

"Do you want to come to Denver with me?" I asked. "I'm staying in a hotel when I'm there, because if I had to stay with my parents I would kill them before the weekend is over." I looked at him from under my lashes and gave him a coy smile. "I reserved a room with a king sized bed."

"Why Joy, are you trying to seduce me?"

So far Luc and I hadn't done more than making out and touching each other with our clothes on. But I was so desperate for him now, I felt like I would die if we didn't have sex soon. In Denver I would have privacy and a real bed, and I wouldn't need to worry about my daughter being in the next room. I didn't have to commit to forever to scratch an itch, right?

Mommy needs some orgasms, I thought to myself with a chuckle.

"I bought some condoms yesterday."

Luc's eyes darkened and I knew his wolf was close to the surface. He was vibrating with coiled energy.

"Are you sure you're ready to take this to the next step Joy? I'm serious about this thing, I'm serious about you, but I don't want to rush into anything until you're ready."

He winced and somehow I knew that his wolf was scratching at his insides.

"I want you Luc," I told him, boldly reaching over to cup his erection. "On a bed. Without worrying about anything besides my pleasure. And yours. I don't know if I believe we're mates, but I believe that we'll be damn good together."

"Well in that case, I hope you bought the jumbo sized box of condoms."

Luc

The next day I left work a few hours early and met up with Joy and Kelsey to head to Denver. Everyone was in good spirits, and we spent a good portion of the two hour drive singing along to Christmas carols that Joy played over the SUV's speakers.

"Hey, did your parents name you Joy because of Christmas?" I asked as "Joy to the World" finished playing.

She did this adorable laugh snort. "Um, no."

"Family name?" I guessed.

She shook her head. "My parents were immigrants and although they spoke English, they had pretty thick accents. They had a hard time conceiving and they'd just about given up on having kids when I finally came along. My dad kept saying that I was 'a joy' over and over so the nurse misunderstood and thought that's what they wanted on the birth certificate. By the time they realized it, it was too late to change it."

I laughed. "You might want to just pretend it's a Christmas thing."

We got to Joy's parents' house a little while later. At her request, I stayed in the car while she dropped Kelsey off. Although her parents greeted Kelsey enthusiastically, they seemed less excited to see their daughter. Joy didn't even go into the house, instead just exchanging a few words with her parents on the porch before kissing Kelsey goodbye and heading back to the car.

She let out a deep breath as we pulled out of the driveway.

I put my hand on her thigh. "Are you OK, Mate?"

She nodded, "Yeah. It's just, that relationship has always been complicated. We never had that easy relationship like you have with your family. Then I moved to Wyoming and married a wolf shifter I'd only known for a few weeks and that drove more of a wedge between us."

"I'm sorry," I told her sincerely. "I know I'm lucky to have got the family I did."

I paused and when she didn't say anything else I decided to change the subject. "Where to next?"

"I have to be at the title company tomorrow at eleven. Until then, I say we check into the hotel, order some room service, and fuck each other's brains out until morning."

My cock jumped to attention at her dirty talk, and so did my wolf.

We are going to claim our mate! Finally!

"Well, I have to say I like this side of you." I growled. "Can you drive faster?"

Less than thirty minutes later we had a keycard in hand and were heading up to our room for the weekend. The minute Joy got the door to our room open, I rushed her inside, slammed the door closed, and was on her like a hungry dog with a bone. Or a wolf, as the case may be.

I backed her against the wall and took her mouth aggressively, my tongue tangling with hers as I fumbled with her clothes.

She must have sensed me unleashing my claws because she pulled back, breathing heavily, and said firmly, "Let's get something clear first. No using your claws to rip up my clothes. I like everything I'm wearing."

I ignored the flare of jealousy that she'd ever been touched by another male, and bit out, "Then get naked. Now."

She pulled her shirt over her head and gave me a challenging gaze. "Bossy, are you?"

I reached down and unzipped her jeans, shoving them down her legs while she took off her bra. "I am an alpha wolf."

She rolled her eyes and giggled. "Does that line work with all the girls?"

I stopped and looked at her, sensing this was important. "What girls?"

"I understand you have quite the playboy reputation in town. I hear you've left a string of broken hearts behind you."

Her voice was teasing, but I recognized the thread of nervousness beneath it. Even though we hadn't fully mated, I'd spent enough time with her that I was starting to be able to tune into her emotions through our developing mate bond.

"My playboy ways are behind me," I answered, meeting her eyes so she could see that I was serious. "The minute I saw you, I was done. I haven't so much as looked at another woman since we met. I love you, Joy. You're my mate."

Her eyes filled with tears, but she held them back. "Don't say that."

"Why not? It's true." I put her hand on my chest, right over my heart. "And I know you can feel the truth in my words."

She stared at our hands for a long moment before visibly shaking herself and pushing on my chest. "Hey! It's not fair that I'm the only one who's naked here. Strip, Mister!"

I removed my clothes in record time then grabbed Joy by the waist and lifted her up onto the nearby dresser. I shoved her legs open and stepped into the cradle of her thighs, my erect cock nudging through the moisture of her slit. Lowering my head, I kissed her deeply, running my hands up and down the smooth skin of her back.

We pulled away to catch our breath, and I grabbed her long hair in one hand, pulling her head to the side and nipping my way down her neck to her shoulder. I sucked the skin into my mouth, adding enough pressure to leave a mark, and she hissed in a breath.

"This is where I'm going to mark you when you agree to be my mate."

"Wait. You would mark me?" she asked with a frown.

I stepped back and looked at her. "Yeah, of course, that's how the world will know that you're my mate. And it's what finalizes the mate bond for us so we can read each other's emotions."

She had the strangest expression on her face, one I couldn't interpret. "What?"

"My ex never wanted to mark me," she explained. "The women in the pack said it was because he didn't love me, and I wasn't worthy to be his mate. When I asked my ex, he said that the mark didn't mean anything because it didn't work with humans. You're saying it does?"

"Yes. I know it does. I heard both Marissa and Sarah talk about it."

She blew out a breath. "In that case, I think he really knew I wasn't his true mate and that's what held him back. I think I was his fallback option. He wouldn't have been able to separate from me as easily if we were fully mated, correct?"

I nodded but didn't respond as my mate processed what she had just learned. In an instant she seemed lighter and more open. I swear I could practically see her walls fall down around us.

"Do I get to mark you?" she asked suddenly. "I mean, if you're going to mark me, it only seems fair."

My wolf pranced happily inside me, understanding as well as I did that our mate had finally accepted us.

"Well, you can try but with your puny human teeth, it might be hard."

She giggled. "I'll show you what I can do with my puny human teeth."

To my surprise she leaned forward and bit my chest. She didn't break the skin, but she sucked hard enough to give me a good-sized hickey that remained visible when she stepped back again. It was one of the hottest things she could have done, and my wolf was ecstatic.

Our mate marks us!

I picked her up bride style and walked over to the large king-sized bed in the center of the room. I set Joy down on her feet, pushed the blankets back, and laid down on my back.

"Get up here!" I ordered, pointing at my face.

"Wait. What?" She looked adorably confused.

"Sit on my face, Mate. I want to taste you."

To my shock, my little mate turned red as a tomato. "I can't do that," she squeaked. "I'm too big."

I looked pointedly at her generous curves, then deepened my voice. "Now."

Her eyes widened, and the room filled with the sweet scent of her arousal as she slowly made her way towards me on the bed. "Don't think you can boss me around outside the bedroom," she warned.

"I wouldn't dream of it," I told her honestly. "Now get on up there."

Joy

I wouldn't say I'd lived a sheltered life. I'd had a handful of lovers over the years before I was married, but never, not once, had a man wanted me to sit on his face. I loved my curves, but the truth was, I was not a small girl.

I couldn't decide whether I was turned on or embarrassed. I straddled Luc's head, holding onto the headboard for balance, and slowly lowered myself towards him. He grabbed my hips and pulled me down until I was literally surrounding him. His long thick tongue licked up my slit and I squeaked.

"You taste delicious, Mate," he growled before returning to his task.

He licked me up and down, sinking deeper into my folds with every pass, until he finally speared his tongue right into my dripping channel. He fucked me with his tongue, and with his hands holding me still, all I could do was go along for the ride.

In an embarrassingly short time, I felt my muscles tighten as my orgasm barreled down on me.

"Luc!" I gasped. "I'm coming."

His tongue slid out of my channel, and he shifted to suck my clit into his mouth. I felt the gentle press of his teeth as he bit down on my swollen bundle of nerves and applied suction at the same time.

"Luc!" I moaned loudly. "Oh fuck!"

My body stiffened and shuddered as I came harder than I'd ever come before in my life. It seemed to go on and on and when it was finally done I sagged against the headboard, completely unworried about smothering Luc with my body. I felt boneless.

Luc lifted me by the hips and shifted my body down so that I was sprawled across his lightly furred chest. He wrapped his strong arms around me, pulling me close.

"Holy crap!" I gasped into his shoulder. "What was that?"

"That was what it's like when you're with your true mate," he told me, his voice thick with satisfaction.

I rolled over with a grown. "You've been very patient. Let's take care of you now."

I slid down the bed until I was face to face with his impressive erection. His cock was long and thick and right now, it looked angry as hell.

"Aw, are you feeling neglected little guy?" I crooned.

"Little guy?" he laughed. "I dare you to say that with your mouth full."

I looked at him through my lashes then lowered my head, taking as much of him into my mouth as I could. He growled, and I saw his claws extend from his fingers and grip the bed sheets.

I moved my mouth up and down him several times, licking around the mushroom tip of his cock and licking up the pre-cum that glistened there. Suddenly Luc grabbed my long hair in his fingers, tugging to get my attention.

"Mate! I need to be inside you."

I let him go with a pop. "So what are you waiting for?" He started to move, and I stopped him with a hand to his chest. "Remember, no glove, no love."

He rolled off the bed with a groan. "Where are those condoms?"

He returned thirty seconds later with a whole strip of them. "Ambitious, are we?" I teased.

He growled and jumped onto the bed. I squealed as he covered me with his huge body, pressing me into the mattress. My sensitive nipples scraped against the hair on his chest as he shifted to give me a long, deep kiss.

When we were both breathless, he pushed back to his knees and rolled the condom onto his thick length. I widened my legs, and he laid down between them, sliding his cock between my dripping folds. He held his upper body up on forearms that were propped on either side of my shoulders and hovered his face above mine.

"Joy, I want to make you my mate," he told me, his voice more serious than I'd ever heard it. "I want to bite you and make you mine. But if you're not ready, we can wait."

I looked into his eyes and somehow I could feel his emotions. I could feel his love for me, the truth of his commitment, the incredible desire he had for me physically. And in that moment, trapped in his gaze, I knew that true mates did exist and that this was meant to be. Somehow my whole life had led up to this moment with this man.

"I want you to fuck me until I can't remember my own name," I told him. "And then I want you to bite me and make me yours forever."

His eyes glowed and with a growl, he plunged inside me in one long stroke. We both moaned as he stilled and gave me some time to adjust to his size.

"Jesus, I feel so full," I bit out. I exhaled long and slow, allowing my muscles to relax, then wrapped my legs around his waist. "Let's do this."

Spurred on by my words, Luc began pounding in and out of me. His pelvis crashed against mine with every push, and I slid up the bed. I reached above my head and braced my palms against the padded headboard to stop the momentum. The move made my breasts lift, and Luc noticed immediately. He lowered his head and took one nipple into his mouth, sucking on my skin as he continued to thrust into my heat. It felt incredible, and every time he bit down on my nipple I felt a zing go all the way down to my core.

"Mate, you taste so good," he gasped before moving to give my other breast the same attention. "Come for me."

He did some kind of a rolling thing with his hips against mine, hitting my clit just right, and I gasped as another orgasm overtook me. I shivered and shook beneath him, chanting his name between gasps.

His thrusts got more erratic, and he sped up, pounding into me roughly.

"I'm close," he grunted.

Luc lowered his head to my neck, pressing his face in the crook of my shoulder. Suddenly he came with a shout, his entire body stiffening above mine for a moment before thrusting into me a few times more.

I felt a sharp bite of pain as Luc bit into the muscles of my upper shoulder. The pain melded with pleasure and impossibly I felt another orgasm rock through my body. I dug my fingernails into his shoulders and pulled him closer as he made me his forever.

I felt a zing of connection and realized that the mate bond was activating. I was immediately more aware of Luc and his emotions, it was the strangest feeling.

Luc pulled out, rolling to rest next to me, licking my wound and wrapping his leg over mine as we both struggled to catch our breath. I felt more alive than I had in my life, the energy pulsing through the mate bond in a way I didn't fully understand but certainly didn't mind.

"I love you, Mate."

He threw one heavy arm over my waist and we both fell into an exhausted sleep.

Luc

"Are you ready to go, Mate?"

I wrapped my arm around Joy's shoulders and gave her a little squeeze. She looked up at me with the sweetest smile. "I hate to leave our little love bubble, but I have to say I really miss my daughter."

"Me too," I answered honestly.

Other than going to the title company and the bank yesterday, we had spent the entire weekend in our hotel room making love so many times I eventually lost count. But after spending so much time with Kelsey the previous week, I'd developed as much love for her as I had for her mom. I missed the little girl too.

Our mate's pup is ours now too, my wolf reminded me.

We checked out of the hotel and headed out of Denver. As we got closer to her parents' house Joy got more and more nervous. Even without my heightened awareness of her through the mate bond I would have been able to pick up on the change in her emotions from her stiff posture and the way she kept tapping her fingers nervously on the steering wheel.

I reached over and palmed her thigh. "What's wrong?"

Joy took a long moment to answer. "This was a great weekend we had together, but I'm just worried about what happens now," she told me honestly. "I think maybe we should keep our relationship a secret for a while."

My head snapped back in surprise and my wolf paced around nervously inside me. "What? Why?"

"I'm nervous how Kelsey is going to react to me dating someone."

"You're doing more than just dating," I growled. "We're mates now."

"I've only been divorced for six months. She might be confused by this whole situation."

I held back a laugh, remembering how when Kelsey and I went to coffee together she told me she wanted me to date her mom. I also knew that once we were around other shifters the secret would be out anyway.

"Is this really about Kelsey?" I asked.

"Sure." She was lying. It might be partly about Kelsey, but that wasn't the whole story.

"Joy." I deepened my voice and gave her thigh a little squeeze. "Can you pull into that restaurant please?"

She pulled the car into the parking lot and put it in park. "Are you hungry?"

"No, I want us to talk about this when you can focus," I responded. "I can tell this is more than just you being worried about Kelsey."

I leaned forward and tapped the mate mark on her neck, and her eyes widened in understanding. "Talk to me. Please."

Her gaze searched mine for a long time, then she sighed deeply.

"When I got together with Cliff, my friends and family were all so appalled. They thought I was crazy, acting irresponsibly. I mean, we moved in together within a month and I got pregnant at the same time, before we were even married. There was a lot of judgement there against me, and distrust against Cliff." Joy stared at her lap, her words were slow and halting.

"Then when I got divorced, everyone was like, 'we told you so, it was too good to last', and even though we were together for six years and people get divorced all the time, it still hurt that people looked at my pain and thought it was what I deserved for foolishly rushing into a relationship."

She looked up, her eyes shiny with tears. "I don't want to go through that again. All the judgement. And I don't want Kelsey to get hurt again if we break up."

"Did you know that most shifters only live for a couple of months after their mate dies?"

She frowned in confusion. "No..."

I placed one hand on each side of her head, looking deep into her eyes, consciously pushing my emotions out to her through our mate bond.

"Now that we're mated, I would literally rather die than be separated from you. There will be no breaking up. I love you Joy, and I love Kelsey and will always treat her like my own. I don't give a single damn about anyone else's opinion about our relationship. You're all that matters, Mate, you and Kelsey."

She moved closer and kissed me softly, her arms wrapping around my shoulders and holding me close. We kissed like we had all the time in the world, and I guess we did. When we pulled apart, she gave me a happy smile.

"Feeling better?"

She nodded.

"Then let's go get my other girl."

Kelsey was waiting for us on the porch when we pulled up into her grandparents' driveway. The little pup had the door open and was sliding into the backseat before Joy or I could even get out of the car.

"Let's go, let's go!" Kelsey demanded as she buckled her seatbelt.

The front door opened, and Joy's mom gave a half-hearted wave before closing the door again. My future mother-in-law was the friendly sort, I thought sarcastically

"How was your time with your grandparents, pup?" I asked Kelsey.

"Terrible," she said with a deep dramatic sigh. "They're boring and mean and they made me go to bed at seven o'clock like I'm some kind of baby. They said I talked too much. And they made me go to church to pray for me to reject my wolf so I can save my soul."

Joy rolled her eyes and suppressed a sigh, clearly annoyed at her parents' behavior. I resolved to not leave the pup alone with her grandparents again in the future and suspected that Joy was doing the same.

"Well, I really missed you baby," Joy told her.

"Thanks Mommy." Suddenly the pup leaned forward as much as her seatbelt would allow and sniffed deeply several times.

"Hey! Something smells different," she said.

She sniffed again. "It's like you both smell like each other. Oh! I know what this means! You are mates now, aren't you?"

Joy slammed on the breaks and violently pulled the car to the side of road. Once the car was in park, she turned to face her daughter. "What did you say?"

"You're mates now, I can tell because your scents are blended together. This is so cool."

Joy looked at me questioningly.

"Shifters can smell the mate bond on other shifters," I confirmed.

"How do you feel about me, um, dating Luc?" Joy asked her daughter.

"I think it's about time," Kelsey said. "I already told Mr. Luc I wanted him to be your boyfriend. I don't understand what took you so long." She sent a reproachful look in my direction like I was the one dragging my feet all this time.

"Are we going to move into Mr. Luc's house now?" she asked.

"We haven't really discussed all that yet sweetie," Joy answered.

"You should. You're going to need his help with the baby, Mommy."

Joy gasped in shock and her eyes widened comically. "Baby? What do you mean?"

I took a sniff and realized what Kelsey had already picked up on. My mate was pregnant. My wolf was ecstatic at this turn of events.

"There's two things you should probably know about shifters," I told my mate. "One, we can smell any changes in hormones, like when someone gets pregnant."

She visibly paled. "Are you saying...? How did this happen? I don't understand, we used..."

I interrupted Joy's sputtering by placing my palm on the soft swell of her belly. "The other thing you should know is that shifters are very virile, particularly the males in my family. We need more than a thin layer latex to stop our swimmers."

"You tell me this now?" she yelped.

I gave her a cocky smile. Despite her surprised reaction, I could sense that my mate was as happy about this development as my wolf and I both were.

"I don't even know what to say right now."

"I know what to say," an amused voice came from the backseat. "This baby better be a girl. Now can we please go home?"

Epilogue – Joy

Nine months later...

"I told you I wanted a sister," Kelsey groused as she looked down at the baby in my arms. "And why is he so red and funny looking?"

Little Matteo – named for Luc's father—scrunched his eyes closed tighter, as if he was blocking out his big sister's words.

Luc swooped in behind Kelsey and picked her up, holding her in his arms like she was the baby, and dancing around the hospital room with her. As she laughed and screeched for him to put her down I couldn't help but compare the difference between this birth and Kelsey's.

Unlike my ex, Luc had been involved in every aspect of my pregnancy, reading books, and attending every appointment with me so he knew what was happening. I knew that the hospital lobby was filled with family members dying to see the new pup. It warmed my heart how welcoming the residents of Greysden had been to me and Kelsey, and now Matteo. Moving here was the best decision I had ever made.

The past nine months had passed in a happy blur. Kelsey and I had moved in with Luc the week after we got back from Denver, and a few months later we had purchased a new, larger home that would accommodate our growing family. The house backed right up onto the woods, and Kelsey and Luc had gotten into the habit of taking their wolves for a run every night before dinner.

It was sweet how they'd bonded over their shifter status. Even sweeter: Kelsey had started calling Luc "Papa". He loved it.

Luc gently set Kelsey down on the bed beside me, and I shifted Matteo into her arms. "There you go sweetie, support his head like we talked about."

She looked down with amazement as the baby's eyes opened and looked right at her. "I guess he's OK," she said grudgingly. The baby gurgled as if he understood her.

Luc squeezed onto the bed by my other side and wrapped his arm around me. "You did good, Mate," he told me, giving me a kiss on the top of my head. "You were so strong and brave."

Honestly, I had been lucky. Despite what doctors called my "advanced age" of thirty-six, the birth had been pretty fast and complication free. The shifter doctor had even commented that I was "pretty strong, for a human."

"They look so sweet together," I said, nodding at our children.

"They sure do," Luc answered. "I can't wait to have another one."

I smacked him in the chest. "Another one? I just gave birth an hour ago, asshole."

He hugged me closer. "I'm just kidding. I love our family just as we are."

"So do I Mate, so do I."

***

Did you like this book? Show the love and leave me a review. Reviews are like puppies, they make you feel happy.

Coming soon: More great instalove romances in the "Holidays with the Shifters" series. In the meantime, keep reading for a special excerpt from "Wolf Doctor", book one of the Bite-Sized Shifters paranormal romantic comedy series.

Special Preview

Wolf Doctor: A Paranormal Romantic Comedy

Twilight. Colt's favorite time of the day.

Stripping off his clothes, he took a deep breath, inhaling the scents on the air. He broke into a run and felt his body change mid-stride. In less than thirty seconds he had transformed from man to wolf.

Muscles and bone lengthening as gray hair sprouted all over his body, almost white in some places. His sharp canine teeth extended from his thickening jaw. He felt his tail grow behind him and he wagged it happily from side to side as he increased his pace, moving so fast his paws seemed to barely touch the ground.

Colt's senses were immediately heightened. His vision was sharper, his ears taking in even the softest sound, and his nose twitched with the wonderful scents of the pristine forest.

He headed through the woods, exhilarating in the feeling of free movement. His wolf loved to run. He hadn't shifted in almost a week. Too long. He needed this. He needed to shift and let his wolf run as much as he needed oxygen or food.

Speaking of food, he could use a snack. He scented a group of hares a mile away and headed in that direction at a gallop. His paws ate up the ground as he tracked the smaller beasts, stopping occasionally to sniff the ground and pick up their trail.

There, up ahead, he saw a flash of fur. He moved quickly, ears pinned back, as his wolf took over, the ultimate predator.

He could smell the fear on the hare as it took off, running for its life. Colt pulled his gums back in a canine smile. He loved the chase. The harder the capture, the better it tasted.

He sped up, following the hare instinctively as it took a sharp turn to the side. He pounced, leaping after the hare. Suddenly his feet hit air. And then he was falling. Fast.

Oh crap. He had overshot and gone right over the edge of the bluff. He could practically feel the stupid hare laughing at him as he tumbled down the embankment, scrambling but unable to stop his downward momentum.

He whined as his body hit the road below with a heavy thump.

Before he could recover he heard the squealing of brakes and suddenly he was airborne again. He landed on the asphalt a second time, feeling bones breaking and muscles tearing. He smelled the scent of his own blood and dimly heard voices as he struggled to stay conscious.

"Oh my god Dennis, you hit that poor dog!" The woman sounded upset.

"I'm not sure that it's a dog Sandy, it might be a wolf," someone, presumably Dennis, responded.

Not a dog, his wolf snipped in his head, clearly offended.

Really, that's your top worry right now? he asked his wolf.

Like all shifters, Colt shared space in his mind with his animal. He and his wolf shared not only the same body, but also the same consciousness.

He noted dimly that the humans who had hit him had exited their truck and were watching him cautiously from where they had stopped. He thought about getting up and whined again. The pain was terrible. It was impossible to move.

"He's bleeding and he's in pain," Sandy said, her voice sounding closer. "We have to get him to the animal hospital."

"There's no way he's going to survive," Dennis answered. "Let me get my shotgun out of the truck and I'll put the poor thing out of his misery."

Colt lifted his head in alarm, although it cost him dearly. He made eye contact with the woman, trying to communicate with her. He tried to make himself look sad and unthreatening. He did not want to die on the side of the road, and he definitely did not want to be put down by some random human with a shotgun. With his luck the guy would be a bad shot and make his injuries even worse.

"NO," Sandy said firmly. "You are not shooting him Dennis. Get the tarp. We'll put him in the back and drive him to the vet."

"He's a wounded animal Sandy," Dennis argued. "He may attack us, especially if he is a wolf."

Sandy continued to hold Colt's gaze. "No, he won't," she replied. "Come on, let's get him some help."

Colt passed out, not knowing who would win their argument. He just hoped it was Sandy.

He did not feel the couple cautiously wrapping him in a tarp and dragging him up into the back of their pick-up. He didn't feel himself sliding around in the truck bed as they raced to the animal hospital. He didn't hear the people loading him onto a gurney and wheeling his large body into the hospital. Both his body and his mind were completely shut down now, blissfully blocking the pain.

Then he felt it. A jolt of happiness and peace.

He opened his eyes, staring through the pain as an angel looked down at him. The overhead light glowed behind her like a halo. Thick brown hair framed her beautiful face. Her eyes were deep brown and impossibly kind.

"What happened?" his angel asked. Her voice made him feel calm. She seemed familiar.

"I think he took a header off a cliff. I think he came rolling down from up above. Suddenly there he was, falling onto the road right in front of us," Dennis explained. "Before I could stop, I hit him with my truck. I didn't do it on purpose, he seemed to come out of nowhere."

The angel's hand dropped gently to his head, rubbing him softly between his ears. He closed his eyes again, pressing against the warmth of her hand and whining softly. He had one thought before he passed out again. *Mate!*

***

For more of Colt and Valerie's story, check out "Wolf Doctor" by Rose Bak. Available now at all major online retailers.

Other Books by Rose Bak

Bite-Sized Shifters Paranormal Romance Series
Wolf Doctor
Kat's Dog
Designer Wolf
Wolf Sheriff
Cocktail Wolf
Holidays with the Shifters
Santa's Claws
Bear Humbug
Jingle Bear
Silver Paws
Joy to the Wolf
The Diamond Bay Contemporary Romance Series
Brand New Penny
Fresh as a Daisy
Right as Rain
The Oliver Boys Band Contemporary Romance Series
Until You Came Along
Rock Star Teacher
Rock Star Writer
Rock Star Neighbor
Loving the Holidays Contemporary Romance Series
Dating Santa
New Year's Steve
Independence Dave
The Good with Numbers Holiday Romance Series
Love Unmasked
The Thanksgiving Scrooge
Maid for Christmas
Countdown to Love

Valentine's Lottery

Reunited Series
Together Again
Finding My Baby
Beach Wedding
Christmas Love Stories
Non-fiction
What to Do If You Find a Cougar in Your Living Room: Self-Care in an Uncaring World
Catch up with these and other stories coming soon. Join my newsletter for more information[1] or follow my author page on your favorite retailer.

---

1.   *https://storyoriginapp.com/giveaways/62ee758e-068f-11eb-904e-c373f6014fe1*

About the Author

Rose Bak has been obsessed with books since she got her first library card at age five. She is a passionate reader with an e-reader bursting with thousands of beloved books.

Although Rose enjoys writing both fiction and nonfiction, romance novels have always been her favorite guilty pleasure, both as a reader and an author. Rose's contemporary romance books focus on strong female characters over age 35 and the alpha males who love them. Expect a lot of steam, a little bit of snark, and a guaranteed happily ever after.

Rose lives in the Pacific Northwest with her family, and special needs dogs. In addition to writing, she also teaches accessible yoga and loves music. Sadly, she has absolutely no musical talent, so she mostly sings in the shower.

Please sign up for Rose's newsletter[1] to get a free book and keep up to date on all the latest news.

---

1. *https://storyoriginapp.com/giveaways/62ee758e-068f-11eb-904e-c373f6014fe1*

Don't miss out!

Visit the website below and you can sign up to receive emails whenever Rose Bak publishes a new book. There's no charge and no obligation.

https://books2read.com/r/B-A-VATM-PZEUB

BOOKS 2 READ

Connecting independent readers to independent writers.

www.ingramcontent.com/pod-product-compliance
Lightning Source LLC
Chambersburg PA
CBHW031500130726
47989CB00003B/1474